Henry the Holiday Pony

Abby ran down the beach. She couldn't wait to see Henry and the donkeys again. Maybe there would even be time for a quick ride before Mr Higgins packed away for the night. She ran past the swing-boats and the ice cream stall and the trampolines.

Suddenly Abby stopped and stared. The beach in front of her was empty.

Mr Higgins, the donkeys – and Henry – had gone!

Titles in Jenny Dale's PONY TALES™ series

1. Sam the School Pony

2. Charlie the Champion Pony

3. Henry the Holiday Pony

4. Freddie the Frisky Pony

5. Lottie the Little Pony

6. Shadow the Secret Pony

7. Rosie the Runaway Pony

8. Willow the Wild Pony

All of Jenny Dale's PONY TALES™ books can
be ordered at your local bookshop or are
available by post from Book Service by Post
(tel: 01624 675137)

Henry the Holiday Pony

by Jenny Dale

Illustrated by Frank Rodgers

A Working Partners Book

MACMILLAN CHILDREN'S BOOKS

Special thanks to Linda Chapman

First published 2000 by Macmillan Children's Books
a division of Macmillan Publishers Limited
20 New Wharf Road, London N1 9RR
Basingstoke and Oxford
www.panmacmillan.com

Associated companies throughout the world

Created by Working Partners Limited
London W6 0QT

ISBN 0 330 37470 2

5 7 9 8 6 4

A CIP catalogue record for this book is available from
the British Library.

Typeset by SX Composing DTP, Rayleigh, Essex
Printed and bound in Great Britain by Mackays of Chatham plc, Kent

Chapter One

"Can I go down to the beach?" Abby Temple asked eagerly.

"What? Now?" said Mr Temple as he carried the two suitcases into the hotel room.

"It's almost six o'clock," Mrs Temple said, putting her bag on the bed. "Why don't you wait till tomorrow, love?"

Abby looked out of the hotel window. Across the road, she could see people walking back from the beach, brightly coloured towels slung over their shoulders, lilos and beach-bags in their hands. Further round, she could see the flashing lights of the swing-boats and the moving horses on the merry-go-round. She felt in her pocket for the packet of mints she had brought from home. "Oh, please let me go. I want to see Henry."

Mrs Temple smiled. "All right," she said. "But don't be long. Remember, supper's at seven o'clock."

As if I could forget, Abby thought

as she ran down the wide staircase, past the familiar TV room and red-carpeted lounge and out through the big glass doors of Fairview Hotel. She and her mum and dad always came to Fairview for their summer holidays. Abby loved it. Outside there was the beach with its fairground rides, sweet stalls and candyfloss. Best of all, there was Henry!

Abby crossed the road outside the hotel and skirted quickly round the stalls. She dodged and swerved around the families, the toddlers and the groups of teenagers.

"Anybody else for a ride?" called the man by the swing-boats.

"Ice creams! Candyfloss! Pink rock!" called out the lady at the sweet stall.

Abby ran on. She dashed past the postcard stand and the trampolines and then she stopped. *There*! Just in front of her, where the stalls and attractions ended, was a line of seven donkeys. At the end of the line was a sandy-coloured pony with a shaggy white mane and tail.

"Henry!" Abby called.

The palomino pony looked round. "Abby!" he whinnied in delight. "You're back!" He stamped in excitement.

Abby raced over. Henry looked as cute as ever. His long forelock fell across his eyes like a heavy

fringe. His tail almost swept the ground. His fancy red and white browband with its ornamental ribbons shone brightly in the sunshine.

Abby put her arms round Henry's neck and hugged him. "I'm glad you're still here!" she said.

"Of course!" snorted Henry,

nuzzling Abby and breathing warm air down the back of her neck. "Where else would I be?"

For the last eight years Henry had belonged to Mr Higgins, the donkey man. Every day in the summer he came out with the donkeys to give children rides along the sand.

Henry snuffled at Abby's hair. He looked forward to Abby arriving for her summer holidays. There were always treats in Abby's pockets and when she rode she didn't pull on the reins or kick her heels against Henry's sides. She just sat still and talked softly.

Abby looked round. Where was Mr Higgins? She spotted the old man carrying a chair and a couple of water buckets across the sand into a small wooden shelter by the road. He was packing away for the night.

Abby fed Henry a mint. "I'm staying for two weeks this year," she told him. "So I can ride you lots!"

The donkeys beside Henry heard the rustle of the sweet paper and pricked their long ears. Abby smiled. "Here's one for you, Jenny, and one for you, Flash," she said, walking along the row and feeding each of the donkeys a mint. She knew all the donkeys by name. But Henry was her favourite.

Mr Higgins came back down the

beach to the donkeys and slowly started to fold up the wooden sign that said *Donkey Rides*. Although it was a hot day he wore a thick coat. As he picked up the sign, he coughed. Henry looked at him anxiously. He had noticed that Mr Higgins had been coughing more than normal in the last few days.

Abby went over. "Hello, Mr Higgins," she said shyly.

Mr Higgins peered at her and then seemed to recognise her. "Hello there," he said. "So you're back again?"

Abby nodded. "I've been saving up my money so I can ride Henry lots this year." She glanced at her watch. Time was passing and she didn't want to make her mum angry on the very first night of the holiday. "I'd better go, Henry," she said, giving the pony a last stroke. "But I'll be here tomorrow."

"I'm glad you're back, Abby!" Henry blew.

"Bye, Mr Higgins!" Abby called as the old man shuffled along the row of donkeys, untying the lead ropes. Abby ran back along the beach. Reaching the trampolines she had one last look over her shoulder. The donkeys and Henry were crowding affectionately around Mr Higgins, nuzzling the old man. Mr Higgins was rubbing their foreheads and murmuring a few words to each. They all looked very happy.

Abby grinned. Tomorrow she would get to ride Henry again. She couldn't wait!

Chapter Two

Abby ate her breakfast as fast as she could the next morning. She didn't want to waste a single moment of her holiday. Pushing away her plate she waited for her mum and dad to finish.

"Now where shall we go today?" Mr Temple said, slowly

spreading a piece of toast with home-made strawberry jam and looking at Mrs Temple. "What about a trip along the coast?"

"But, Dad!" Abby exclaimed. "I want to . . ." Suddenly she saw the look in her dad's eyes and stopped. She was being teased.

"Go on then," her mum said, smiling at her. "You can go down to the beach. Dad and I will come and find you when we've finished breakfast. But don't go into the sea until we're there."

"I won't!" Abby rushed out and ran down the steps of the hotel. She had saved enough money for three rides each day. She wondered whether she should pay for all three rides at once and

have an extra long go or whether
she should spread the rides out
through the day. It was a very
difficult decision!

The beach was just starting to fill
up with people. Abby saw that Mr
Higgins was leading a little girl
up and down the beach on one of
the donkeys. Henry and the other
donkeys were munching happily
at a pile of hay.

"Henry!" Abby called.

Henry looked up. "Abby!" he
whinnied. "Have you come to ride
me?"

Abby ran up and patted him.
After a bit, Mr Higgins came over.

"Hi, Mr Higgins," Abby said.
She frowned. The old man didn't
look very well. He was breathing

heavily and his face was pale.

"Morning, lass," Mr Higgins said, smiling faintly. "Have you come to ride Henry then?"

"Yes, please!" Abby said. She felt the money in her pocket. "I think I'll have two rides now, please," she said. "And then one later." She gave Mr Higgins her money.

Mr Higgins led Henry out and

18

held the reins while Abby mounted.

Abby patted Henry. "Come on, boy."

"Here we go!" Henry neighed. Abby grinned. It was brilliant to be riding Henry again. "Should we trot?"

Henry snorted. "Yes, please."

Abby felt Henry pulling at the reins. "OK then, boy," she said, squeezing with her heels. They trotted out to the plastic traffic cone that marked the end of the ride and then turned round and trotted back.

"This is fun!" snorted Henry. Normally he only got to walk.

At the cone, Abby slowed Henry down. "We'll walk back," she

said. She wanted to make the ride last as long as possible.

As Henry walked back across the sands, Abby stroked his mane. It was full of tangles. Abby frowned.

"Did you enjoy yourself?" Mr Higgins asked.

"Yes!" Abby said, as she dismounted. "Thanks, Mr Higgins!"

A small queue of children had gathered. The next person in the line, a boy, hurried forward. "Is it my turn now?" he asked.

"See you later, Henry," Abby said, giving Henry a last pat as Mr Higgins took the reins and the boy put his foot in the stirrup. She stepped back as Henry was led away across the sand. She wished she could ride Henry all day long. She felt for her money. At least she had enough left for one more ride.

"Abby!" Hearing her name being called, Abby turned round. Her mum and dad were walking towards her. They were carrying two beach chairs and a sun umbrella. "Did you have a nice ride?" her mum asked. "We saw you trotting."

Abby nodded.

"We were wondering where to put these," Mr Temple said, looking at the chairs under his arm.

"Can we put them near here?" Abby asked.

Her mum and dad agreed. Soon

the chairs and the umbrella were all set up. While her mum sunbathed and her dad read the newspaper, Abby sat on the sand and watched Henry being ridden up and down. After a bit Mr Higgins brought Henry back to the line and tied him up so that he could have a rest.

Abby went over. She took the packet of mints out of her pocket and offered Henry one. "Here, Henry."

"Yummy!" snorted Henry, crunching the mint with his teeth.

Abby noticed again that Henry's mane was tangled, and his coat was a little dirty. She tried to smooth it down with her hands. "You're a bit untidy today,

Henry," she said. She saw a grooming brush lying on the ground. Maybe she could give Henry a brush over? Abby ran up to Mr Higgins who was untying Patch, a donkey with a white splodge on her neck. "Would you like me to groom Henry for you, Mr Higgins?" she asked.

Mr Higgins looked surprised. "Groom Henry? But wouldn't you rather be playing on the beach?"

Abby shook her head.

"Well, that would be a real help then, lass," Mr Higgins said. He coughed. "I haven't been feeling so good lately."

"Excuse me!" A lady from the queue called. "I think it's my son's turn next."

Mr Higgins led Patch over to the little boy who was waiting. Abby eagerly ran back to Henry. She picked up the brush and groomed Henry all over. By the time she had finished, she was hot and dusty but Henry's mane was tangle-free and his golden coat was shining.

"Thank you," whinnied Henry. "That feels much better!" He nuzzled Abby affectionately.

Abby wiped her arm across her forehead and looked at the donkeys. They could all do with a brush too. She set to work. This was loads better than playing on the beach!

As it got nearer lunchtime the queue for rides grew shorter and shorter. At last, there was no one

left waiting and Mr Higgins came over to Abby. "You're doing a grand job," he said, looking at the donkeys and Henry.

Abby looked at him eagerly. "Can I come and help you every day?" She saw the surprise on Mr Higgins's face. "It's fun!"

Mr Higgins smiled. "So you really like donkeys and ponies then, lass?"

Abby nodded. "I wish I could have a pony." She sighed. "But Mum and Dad say they're too expensive."

"Tell you what," Mr Higgins said. "I'll give you a free ride on Henry for every donkey you groom. How does that sound?"

"Brilliant!" gasped Abby.

Henry stamped a hoof in approval.

Mr Higgins coughed. "It's a deal then." He smiled. "Now, how about a quick ride before lunch?"

"Yes, please!" Abby cried.

After she had ridden Henry, Abby raced back to her mum and dad to tell them the news. They smiled.

"Just remember to tell Mr Higgins that you won't be here at the weekend," Mrs Temple said.

Abby suddenly remembered that they were going to stay with Auntie Carol for the weekend. "Can't I stay here?" she asked.

Mrs Temple laughed. "What? On your own? Don't be silly!"

Abby felt a bit disappointed that she had to go away but at least it was only for a couple of days. She would still have all the next week with Henry and the donkeys before he had to go home.

For the next few days, Abby had a brilliant time. Grooming all seven donkeys and Henry each day

meant that she got eight free rides
– as well as the three that she paid
for. She didn't think she had ever
had a better holiday!

Henry whinnied to Abby every
morning as she came running
along the beach. On Friday
morning, he whinnied and then
snorted in surprise. Abby wasn't
wearing her usual old shorts and
trainers. She looked much smarter.

Abby patted Henry. "I can't
come and groom you today,
Henry," she explained. "I've got to
see my auntie. We're going to stay
with her for the weekend."

Abby looked around. It was a
cloudy morning and the beach
was quiet. Mr Higgins was sitting
in his chair, his coat pulled tightly

around him. He was coughing
again. Abby wondered whether
Henry and the donkeys would get
groomed at all while she was
away. "Oh well," she said,
stroking Henry, "I'll be back soon
and give you all a really good
brush then."

Henry snorted and looked
anxiously at Mr Higgins. He

didn't think the old man looked at all well. He nudged Abby and blew in her face. "Do you think he's all right?" he snorted.

Just then, Mrs Temple appeared on the beach. "Abby!" she called. "We've got to go!"

"Bye, Mr Higgins!" Abby called. The old man lifted a hand and smiled faintly.

Abby put her arms around Henry's neck. "Bye then, Henry," she said. "See you late on Sunday."

Henry nuzzled her hair and neck, his warm breath tickling Abby's skin. He had a horrible worried feeling inside. Suddenly he didn't want Abby to go. He rested his head on Abby's shoulder.

"I'll miss you, Henry," Abby whispered.

"Come on, Abby!" Mrs Temple called impatiently.

Abby reluctantly tore herself away.

"Goodbye!" Henry whinnied, watching Abby run off along the sands.

Abby and her parents got back to the hotel on Sunday afternoon. As soon as her dad had parked the car, Abby leaped out. She wanted to go and see Henry.

"Don't be long!" Mrs Temple called.

"I won't!" Abby yelled. She ran down to the beach. She'd had a good time at her auntie's but she couldn't wait to see Henry and the donkeys again. Maybe there would even be time for a quick ride before Mr Higgins packed away for the night. She ran past the swing-boats and the ice cream stall and the trampolines. Suddenly Abby stopped and stared. The beach in front of her was empty.

Mr Higgins, the donkeys – and Henry – had *gone*!

Chapter Three

Abby looked around the vast, empty space of beach. What had happened? Where were the donkeys? Seeing the trampoline man standing by his wooden hut, Abby ran over to speak to him. "Please!" she gasped. "Do you know where Mr Higgins and the donkeys have gone?"

The trampoline man had blue tattoos on his arms and a bald head. "You're the girl who was helping the old man with his donkeys last week, aren't you?" he asked. Abby nodded. "Poor Mr Higgins," the trampoline man said. "It was dreadful."

Abby felt a stab of fear. "What's happened?" she asked.

"You haven't heard?' the trampoline man said. Abby shook her head. "Well, Mr Higgins collapsed on Friday afternoon," the man explained. "I was over here when I suddenly heard that pony of his whinnying. I looked round and there Mr Higgins was, just lying on the ground. Of course, I called an ambulance straight away. They took him off to hospital."

Abby was horrified. "Is Mr Higgins all right?"

The man nodded. "He's still in hospital at the moment but they think he's going to be OK. He's going to be weak for a while though. When he gets out he'll need to take things more easily. The social services are going to arrange for him to move into a special flat where there'll be someone around to keep an eye on him."

"But what about the donkeys?" Abby asked quickly. She knew their field was attached to Mr Higgins's house.

"He won't be able to look after them any more," the man said. "I heard they've been taken to a horse and donkey sanctuary." He sighed and shook his head. "The beach isn't going to be the same without them."

Abby was so shocked she couldn't speak. She walked slowly towards the empty space where the donkeys had stood. She could hardly believe it. No donkeys! No Henry! They had all gone to a sanctuary. *A sanctuary*! Suddenly Abby realised what that meant – if Henry was at a sanctuary then Abby might never see him again.

She ran back to the trampoline man. "Please!" she gasped. "Do you know where the sanctuary is – the one the donkeys have gone to?"

The trampoline man shook his head. "Sorry."

Abby looked round. Maybe someone else would know. She ran over to the man by the swing-boats. "Excuse me!" she cried. "Do you know the name of the sanctuary that Mr Higgins's donkeys were taken to?"

The man shook his head. "No, sorry."

Abby ran on to speak to the teenager who looked after the merry-go-round, but he couldn't help either – nor could the lady at the postcard stall. Abby began to feel desperate. What if she never saw Henry again!

"Abby?"

Abby turned. Her dad was walking towards her.

"I was just coming down to find you," Mr Temple said. "You've been gone ages." He frowned. "What's the matter?"

"It's Mr Higgins!" Abby exclaimed. Tears welled up in her eyes as she explained the whole story. "It's so terrible and now I'm never going to see Henry again! No one knows where he's gone!" She brushed away her tears with the back of her hand.

Abby's dad put an arm around her shoulder. "We'll find out somehow. I'll ask around tomorrow – someone must know." He looked round. "Come on. How about an ice cream to cheer you up?"

Abby shook her head. She was far too upset to want an ice cream. But her dad was already walking over to the stall. "What do you want?" he called. "A cone or an ice lolly?"

Abby ran after him. "I don't want anything, Dad! I just want to

find out where Henry and the donkeys are!"

"Excuse me?"

Abby looked up. The ice cream lady was leaning over the counter towards him. "Are you talking about Mr Higgins's donkeys?"

Abby nodded.

The ice cream lady smiled. "I think I might be able to help."

Chapter Four

"I was the one who rang the sanctuary and asked them to take the animals," the ice cream lady explained. "It's the pony and donkey sanctuary near West Marton. About two miles down the coast."

Abby turned to her dad. "Can

we go there?" she asked eagerly. "Tomorrow?"

Mr Temple nodded. "Of course." He looked gratefully at the ice cream lady. "Thank you."

"A pleasure," the lady said, smiling. "It's such a shame. Mr Higgins was devoted to those donkeys. I don't know how he'll cope without them." She sighed. "Poor man. He lived all by himself in that damp, old cottage. No wonder he became ill." She smiled at Abby. "If you see those donkeys give them a pat from me. I always thought they livened the beach up. This place will certainly be different without them."

Abby walked slowly back to the hotel with her dad. She felt a bit happier now she knew where Henry was. But she couldn't help thinking about poor Mr Higgins. It was so sad. He would miss his donkeys so much, and they would miss him. Abby knew how much they – and Henry – had loved the old man. If only there was something she could do.

Abby didn't sleep very well that night. "Can we go to the sanctuary now?" she asked as soon as breakfast was over.

Her mum nodded.

They drove out of the hotel car park. Along the beach the stalls were just opening up and people were starting to make their way down to the sand.

Suddenly, Abby stared. "Look!" she exclaimed. "It's Mr Higgins!"

"You're right," her mum said. "What's he doing? Surely he should still be in hospital."

The old man was standing by his wooden shelter. He was looking sadly down at the empty space of beach where his donkeys had once been. His thick coat was wrapped around his shoulders and he looked frail and lonely.

Mr Temple stopped the car. Abby jumped out and ran over to Mr Higgins. Her mum and dad followed more slowly.

"Hello, Mr Higgins," Abby said shyly when she reached the old man.

Mr Higgins turned in surprise.

Seeing Abby, he managed a faint
smile. "Why, hello, lass," he said.

"Are you feeling better now?"
Abby asked.

Mr Higgins nodded. "But life
won't be the same without Henry
and the donkeys." He looked
sadly out at the beach. "You know,
they weren't just animals to me.
They were my friends."

Abby bit her lip. She wished there was something she could do. Just then her mum and dad came up.

"Hello, Mr Higgins," her mum said. "How are you?"

"I've been better," the old man said, coughing.

"But surely you should still be in hospital," Mrs Temple said, looking at him in concern.

"I didn't want to stay there," Mr Higgins replied. "I left early. I wanted to find out how the donkeys and Henry were." He stared out at the beach. "Sixty years I've been looking after donkeys on this beach – sixty years, and now they're gone." He swallowed. "I didn't even get a chance to say goodbye."

Abby had an idea. "We're going to the sanctuary," she said quickly. "Where Henry and the donkeys are. Would you like to come, Mr Higgins?" She looked at her mum and dad. They were nodding.

"You're more than welcome to," Mr Temple said.

Mr Higgins stared at them, his face lighting up with pleasure. "Go and see my donkeys and Henry? Why, that would be wonderful!"

Mrs Temple smiled. "Well, what are we waiting for? The car's just over there."

Chapter Five

The sanctuary was set back from the road, up a little track. From the car park it was impossible to see much. Abby followed her parents and Mr Higgins up to the ticket office by the entrance. A queue had formed – lots of tourists were visiting the sanctuary.

Outside the door of the ticket office a young man wearing a metal badge that said *Manager* was talking to a girl in jeans who had three head collars in her hands. "Sorry, I can't come and help," he said. "Someone's got to run the ticket office. We've got loads of visitors today." He ran a hand through his hair. "You'll just have to deal with them!"

'But they're impossible to catch," the girl said. "And they're really mean – one of them even tried to kick me!"

Mr Temple got to the ticket office window. The manager turned and smiled quickly at him. "Sorry about this, sir. I'll be with you in just a minute." He turned back to the girl. "Look, I'll come and help when I can." The girl walked away. The man turned back to Mr Temple. "Four tickets, is it, sir?"

Mr Temple nodded. "It looks like we've caught you at a busy time," he said as he handed the manager the money.

The man nodded. "We've just

lost a member of staff and at the weekend we had some new donkeys and a pony in, which are being rather difficult to handle. They don't seem to be settling in very well."

Abby and Mr Higgins looked at each other.

"New donkeys and a pony?" Mr Higgins said. "Are they the ones from the beach?"

"That's right, sir."

"They were *mine*," Mr Higgins said, coughing.

The manager stared in surprise. "Are you Mr Higgins? The donkey man?"

Mr Higgins nodded. "Aye, that's right."

Abby could see that they were

going to talk for some time. But she wanted to see Henry.

Leaving Mr Higgins and her mum and dad at the ticket desk, she hurried through the gate that led into the sanctuary.

A long gravel pathway stretched straight ahead and on either side were green fields filled with ponies and donkeys. On each gate there was a board with lots of information about the animals.

Abby's eyes searched across the fields. Suddenly she saw what she was looking for. In a field with about five other ponies and all the beach donkeys was *Henry*!

Abby raced down the gravel path to the field gate. She stopped. The notice-board on the gate said,

New Arrivals. Please do not enter.

"Henry!" Abby shouted. "Henry, I'm here!"

Henry looked up from the grass. His ears pricked as far forward as they would go. "Abby!" he whinnied in delight. He galloped over, his mane and tail flying.

He screeched to a stop. "I never thought I'd see you again!" he neighed, putting his head over the fence.

Abby flung her arms around Henry's neck. "Oh Henry!" she cried. "I'm so glad we found you!"

Henry blew warm kisses over Abby's face and hair. "I've missed you," he snorted. "Why have they brought us here?" Suddenly his head shot up. Walking along the gravel path with Abby's mum and dad and the manager was a person he knew and loved better than anyone in the world. "Mr Higgins!" he whinnied shrilly. "Mr Higgins!"

"Henry!" Mr Higgins called back. Hearing the sound of his voice,

Mr Higgins's donkeys all lifted their heads. They all started braying and, within seconds, they were thundering down to the gate.

Mr Higgins hurried forward, a new spring in his step. "Jenny! Flash! Patch!" he cried. He reached the gate and started to undo the bolt. "Sam! Thunder! Socks!"

"Mr Higgins!" The manager was looking rather anxious. "Mr Higgins, all the animals in that field are new to us. Please don't go in there. They're very unsettled and you might get hurt."

But Mr Higgins took no notice. He opened the gate and went into the field. The donkeys and Henry crowded round him, pushing and shoving to get close.

Mr Higgins gently murmured a few words to each donkey. As his hands rested lightly on their foreheads, the pushing and shoving stopped as if by magic. The donkeys and Henry stood quietly, content to blow down

their nostrils and nuzzle their master. The other ponies in the field walked curiously over to see what was happening. As Mr Higgins spoke to them, they also became quiet.

The manager watched, openmouthed. "You certainly know how to calm them," he said, staring as if he couldn't believe his eyes.

Mr Higgins smiled at him. "Let's just say I speak their language." He gave each of the donkeys and ponies a pat and then left the field.

"That's amazing!" the manager said, as the ponies and donkeys crowded around the gate.

Mr Higgins looked sadly at his donkeys and Henry. "I guess this really is goodbye." He turned to go.

Abby looked desperately at her mum and dad.

"No!" Henry whinnied.

Suddenly the manager put his hand on Mr Higgins's arm. "Mr Higgins, you . . . er . . . wouldn't be looking for a job, by any chance, would you?" he asked.

Mr Higgins stopped. He stared in surprise. "A job?"

"We're really short-staffed at the moment," the manager explained. "We need someone who can work with the new donkeys and ponies when they arrive. It often takes a while for them to settle in, and we need someone with experience to work with them. I was going to advertise tomorrow but after seeing what you did just now – well . . ." He smiled. "If you want it, the job's yours."

"Mr Higgins! That would be wonderful!" Abby exclaimed.

"It would mean living here," the manager said quickly. "But the work is very flexible and we have a cottage on site. It's small but quite warm, with central heating." He looked at Mr Higgins. "I don't know if you'd be interested in thinking about it?"

Mr Higgins's face creased into a huge smile. "I don't need to think about it! Give me a couple of weeks to get completely fit and then I'll take it!" He shook his head in delight. "A job here, with all my donkeys and Henry. What more could I possibly want?"

The donkeys brayed excitedly and Henry whinnied. "We don't have to say goodbye after all!" he neighed.

While the manager talked to Mr Higgins about the job and cottage, Abby went over to stroke Henry. "I wish I didn't have to say goodbye to you," she said. "I'll miss you, Henry."

Henry nuzzled her. "I'll miss you too, Abby."

Abby's mum came up and put an arm around Abby's shoulders. "We can come and visit whenever we're down here, love."

Abby nodded. But she knew that it wasn't going to be the same.

Mr Temple was reading the
notice-board on the gate of the
next-door field. "It says here that
the sanctuary runs an adopt-a-
pony scheme," he said. "If you
pay them some money you get a
certificate and a photograph and a
regular letter telling you how your
pony is doing." He looked at
Abby's face and smiled. "Do you
think they'll let you adopt
Henry?"

Abby stared at him. "Adopt
Henry?" she gasped.

The manager overheard them.
"I'm sure we can arrange for you
to adopt him if you want."

"Yes, please!" Abby exclaimed.

The manager smiled. "Well,
when you've finished having a

look around come to my office
and I'll see what we can sort out."

Abby turned to Henry. "Do you
hear that, Henry?" she cried. "I'm
going to adopt you!" She flung
her arms round Henry's neck.
"That makes you almost mine!"

"That's fine by me, Abby!"
whickered Henry. He blew

happily into Abby's hair. "Just fine!"

Mrs Temple smiled. "And if you like, when we go home, I'll get in touch with the riding school and see if they'll let you help down there at the weekends and in the holidays. Then you can learn to ride properly."

'Yes, please!" cried Abby. She hugged Henry in delight. "Oh, Henry, everything's worked out perfectly, after all!"